A Candle
for Christmas

BY Jean Speare
ILLUSTRATED BY Ann Blades

Douglas & McIntyre

VANCOUVER/TORONTO

Tomas woke with a start. The sheets on his bed were cold and he shivered. Then he remembered that he was staying at Nurse Roberta's, not in his own house. At home in his bed, rolled up in rough gray blankets instead of sheets, he never felt cold. He would have been much cozier in his thick balbriggan underwear, but "No, no," said Nurse Roberta, "into pajamas with you." She had fluttered around like a bird.

The gray morning light filtered through the frosted windowpane and lay like ice on the polished linoleum floor. At home the morning light spread across rough-sawed boards and looked golden and inviting to his feet. Tomas leaned out of bed. With one arm, he pulled his moccasins from under the bed and placed them so he could step right into them. He must get up.

"Good morning, Tomas." Nurse Roberta smiled cheerfully. His own "Good morning" was lost in a clatter of utensils as Nurse threw herself into making breakfast.

"There now. Come on, get your toast and cocoa. See, see," she said, pushing the toast rack toward him. "Each piece is just like a brown mooley cow in its stall, soaked with butter. And here's the jam. It's a cold morning. Forty below. Drink your cocoa. You'll need a second cup."

When breakfast was eaten, Nurse Roberta said, "Now into your sweater, your jacket, your cap, and your mitts. Now your scarf." He knew perfectly well how to put them on by himself, but Nurse Roberta liked helping him. He stood still while she pulled and tugged at them.

"It's Christmas Eve tonight," he said through the muffles of scarf.

"Yes, it is," Nurse replied.

"Do you think they will be back?" he asked.

Nurse was thoughtful for a moment. "Yes," she answered slowly, "I'm sure they will be back. Your father said they would be, and they will."

Tomas walked up the road toward the school. He could see the reservation stretched out before him, smoke rising from many stovepipes into the cold clear air. His father and mother had been gone nearly two weeks now, far over the hills to their cattle range. In the winter's cold, with deep snow and north winds, it would take a long time to get there and back. The horses, pulling a heavy sleigh, would soon tire from breaking the trail.

"We *have* to go, Tomas," his father had said. "Uncle Alphonse must be in real trouble or he would have come in for his Christmas supplies long ago. I may need your mother's help. But we won't be gone longer than a week. I promise."

His mother had kissed him and held him close. "We hate to leave you, but Nurse Roberta loves to have you visit. You'll have a good time with her, and we'll be back in lots of time for Christmas, you'll see."

School was long and boring today. Tomas could not keep his mind on his spelling or the long columns of figures the teacher wrote on the board.

Finally at three o'clock the school bell rang loudly, proclaiming the Christmas holidays. School books were slammed shut, papers and notebooks jammed recklessly into classroom desks, while the teacher wished the students a Merry Christmas. Tomas rushed out the door with his scarf streaming from one hand. He raced down the road to Nurse Roberta's house.

He ran up the back porch steps two at a time, flung open the kitchen door, and skidded across the floor in his snow-covered boots.

"Have they come?" he asked Nurse Roberta, who was rolling bandages at a big worktable.

"Not yet, Tomas."

Tomas crossed to the window and scratched a hole in the frost. He melted the rime by blowing hot breath on it from deep in his throat, then scratched some more. He kneeled, looking out through the hole for a long time, so long that Nurse thought he must be seeing something.

"What are you looking at?" she asked. "Can you see your parents?"

"No. They won't get home for Christmas. I just know they won't..."

"Come over here," Nurse said cheerfully. "It's time to wrap the gifts for your parents while I make our supper. The paper is there and you can use gauze for ribbon. Come on, now."

Tomas wrapped the knife sheath and beaded headband he had made. Then he tied each one with hospital gauze which made a bow like a small snowdrift.

"I have a surprise for you," Nurse said. No matter how he coaxed her, she would not tell him what it was.

As soon as supper was over and the dishes were cleared away, Nurse Roberta changed into pants and they wrapped themselves in their warmest clothes. Nurse pushed the gifts into her pockets, then pointed to a huge box by the door.

"You carry that, Tomas."

Tomas wondered if he would be able to lift it, but when he did, it was almost as if nothing were inside.

"Is this the surprise?" he asked.

"Part of it," Nurse replied as they went out into the winter twilight.

A snow road took them down a long hill between many small houses whose yellow windows were little more than dim smudges in the evening light and whose ribbons of smoke tapered straight up into the sky. Tomas was dying of curiosity. He shook the box as he followed Nurse. All he could hear was a rustle.

As they drew closer to his house, Tomas saw a dark shape by the door.

"A tree!" he exclaimed.

"Yes, a Christmas tree—a beautiful tree. Benjamin cut it for us. What do you think of that!"

"Are we going to take it inside and decorate it?"

"Indeed we are. And what do you think is in the box?"

"The decorations!" he said.

They wrestled the tree into the cabin and stood it and the box in a corner. The cabin was cold, although red embers still glowed in the drum heater from a fire Nurse had banked early in the morning. Tomas put some logs in the stove and then leaned down and blew as hard as he could on the coals. Eager little flames began to curl up over the fresh wood. Soon warmth spread out into the room.

They got to work hanging the beautiful ornaments on the branches of the tree. Nurse sang carols and with each small piece of glass and tinsel, the tree grew lovelier.

Suddenly there was a frantic knocking at the door. Before Nurse could answer a man burst in. "My baby is sick. He's coughing very badly," he said. "We can't stop him. Can you come? Please come right away."

Nurse quickly wrapped herself in her coat and scarf.

"Tomas, I'll come back for you as soon as I can." She was part way out the door when she turned. "Be very careful and keep the stove going so you'll stay warm."

Tomas walked around the room. He found a candle by the door set in a narrow-necked jar. If I blow out the lantern and light the candle, the tree will look even more beautiful, he thought. And he imagined how the candle would reflect in all the ornaments.

But first he went to the heater, piled more wood on the coals and opened the damper. Then he lit the candle and blew out the lantern. Sitting on the floor near the crackling fire, he looked at the tree. Sure enough, there were a thousand candles glittering and dancing in the ornaments.

In a little while he stood up. He must get more logs from outside.

It was dark and snow covered the woodpile. He carried the candle with him and set it on the windowsill where the eaves protected it from the wind and gusting snow.

The candlelight danced in the night and Tomas got to work. He had forgotten his cap and scarf and mitts, so he had to be quick. He swept the snow off the woodpile and used the big axe to separate the logs, which had frozen together, the way his father had shown him. With the little axe, he split some wood into smaller pieces for kindling. Then he carried it all inside the house, two and three logs at a time until the woodbox was full and there was extra kindling piled beside it on the floor.

Tomas warmed his hands by the red-hot side of the stove. It felt good. His fingers and feet tingled. His face glowed and the snow that had blown into his hair started to melt and trickle down his neck and cheeks. He turned down the damper, so the logs would burn more slowly.

I wish my mom and dad were here, he thought as he curled up on the foot of the bed. The wind whined around the corners of the cabin. The burning wood crackled and snapped. The candle flickered brightly outside where Tomas had forgotten it. His eyes closed and he fell asleep. As he slept, he dreamed of the candle.

Tomas saw himself walking down the sleigh road. There stood the candle before him. It was every bit as tall as he was.

It grew taller and taller until the flame reached far into the sky and turned the falling snowflakes into sparks. The tallest trees seemed no higher than blades of grass beside it. It lit up the snow-covered hills.

In his dream, Tomas heard Nurse Roberta's voice softly calling, "Tomas, Tomas." Cattle bawled and bells rang, the kind his father put on the horses' harness in wintertime.

Tomas jerked awake. "The candle!" he exclaimed, tumbling off the bed. He pulled on his boots and dashed outside. The candle was still burning brightly on the windowsill. Tomas grabbed it and ran back inside.

His mother and father were standing in the cabin. "You're home!" he shouted.

"Yes, son, we are," his father said. "You rushed out in such a hurry you didn't see us! We're all here—your mother, Uncle Alphonse, and the cattle."

"All the cattle?" said Tomas.

"Uncle Alphonse broke his leg and wolves were killing off the yearlings. We couldn't leave them out there. It's been a long hard drive, but we brought them all back. And Uncle Alphonse is resting at Nurse Roberta's."

"You can put this down now," his mother said, taking the candle from Tomas's hand and setting it on the table.

"I left the candle outside on the windowsill when I was chopping wood," Tomas explained. "Then I fell asleep and dreamed that it grew so big that it could light your way home."

"That's strange," his mother said. "Tonight when the going was at its very worst and your father could hardly keep the herd on the road behind me as I drove the team, I thought about you. We must get home for Christmas. We promised Tomas, I thought. The more I thought of you, the brighter the road seemed."

"*You* thought about *me*," said Tomas, "and *I* was thinking about *you*."

"And the more I wanted to get home to you," his mother said, "the brighter and clearer the way became. The horses were floundering in the snow, but they found the road again and started pulling homeward. Your father came up on his horse and said, 'Those must be the village lights ahead.' They were. The next thing we knew we were home."

Tomas snuggled close to his mother and father. "I'm so glad you got here in time. You said you would be home for Christmas, and here you are."